Anna Dean

Meggie's Magic

illustrated by

Colin Stevens

Viking
Penguin Books Australia Ltd
487 Maroondah Highway, PO Box 257
Ringwood, Victoria, 3134, Australia
Penguin Books Ltd
Harmondsworth, Middlesex, England
Viking Penguin, A Division of Penguin Books USA Inc.
375 Hudson Street, New York, New York 10014, USA
Penguin Books Canada Limited
10 Alcorn Avenue, Toronto, Ontario, Canada M4V 1E4
Penguin Books (N.Z.) Ltd
182-190 Wairau Road, Auckland 10, New Zealand

First published by Penguin Books Australia, 1992
10 9 8 7 6 5 4 3 2 1
Copyright © Anna Dean, 1992
Illustrations Copyright © Colin Stevens 1992

Typeset in Bembo by Leader Composition
Made and printed in Hong Kong by Book Builders

Illustration technique: acrylic paints on hardboard panels.

National Library of Australia
Cataloguing-in-Publication data:
Dean, Anna, 1951-
Meggie's magic

ISBN 0 670 82761 4.

I. Stevens. Collin. II. Title.
A823.3

Meggie's Magic

Anna Dean

illustrated by

Colin Stevens

VIKING

For Christopher, Emma, Anthony and all their magic.
A.D.
For Emmett, Emma and the Norman Family.
C.S.

When Meggie was eight years old, she got very sick and died.

Now there's just Mummy, Daddy and me.

Mummy can't talk about
Meggie without crying.
Daddy goes for long walks
to think about things.
I try to keep them company.

They miss Meggie very much.

I miss Meggie too.

She was my sister and my best friend.

We had a secret place

where we would hide if we were in trouble.

It was our place to talk about
special things too,
and play special games.
It was filled with our magic.

I went there today when I was feeling lonely.

The magic was still there.

It wasn't just the ballet shoes we danced in for the Queen,

or the spider webs we used to trap fairies.

It wasn't even Midnight, our witch's cat,
who breathed magic into all our brews,

or the gowns and jewels we wore to dazzle
princes and knights of old.

It was an inside kind of magic.

It was our secrets, our dreams,
our night-time shivers, all the
things we shared that I'd
tucked away inside me.

I was filled with Meggie's magic.
I guessed Mummy and Daddy must be
filled with Meggie's magic too.

And you know what that means . . .

It means that Meggie's magic didn't die.
I can't wait to tell them!